Emma Thomson's

felicity Wishes

Spooky Sleepover

and other stories

By Helen Bailey and Emma Thomson
Illustrated by Emma Thomson

Hodder
Children's
Books

A division of Hachette Children's Books

How to make your felicity Wishes.

W I S H

With this book comes an extra special wish for you and your best friend.

Hold the book together at each end and both close your eyes.

Wriggle your noses and think of a number under ten.

Open your eyes, whisper the numbers you thought of to each other.

Add these numbers together. This is your

✫ Magic Number ✫

you

best friend

Place your little finger on the stars, and say your magic number out loud together. Now make your wish quietly to yourselves. And maybe, one day, your wish might just come true.   Love

felicity

x

For my mum and dad, Betty and Roy.
E.V.T

For my parents, Eileen and George,
and my brother, John.
H.E.B

Emma Thomson's
felicity Wishes®

FELICITY WISHES
Felicity Wishes © 2000 Emma Thomson
Licensed by White Lion Publishing

Spooky Sleepover text © 2002 Helen Bailey and Emma Thomson
Illustrations copyright © 2002 Emma Thomson

First published in Great Britain in 2002 for WHSmith
This edition published 2005

A Catalogue record for this book is available from the British Library

ISBN-10: 0 340 90298 1
ISBN-13: 978 0 340 90298 1

Printed in China.

Hodder Children's Books
A division of Hachette Children's Books, 338 Euston Road, London NW1 3BH

CONTENTS

Swimming Secrets

The weather in Little Blossoming
was glorious. Felicity and her friends
were sitting in the sunshine on the
front step of Polly's house, warming
their wings in the early summer sun.

"Ooh, this is lovely," said Felicity,
stretching out her legs and letting

one of her shoes drop off. "Summer is *definitely* on its way!"

"The weather forecast said that summer would be here by the weekend," said Daisy. "It's going to get hotter and hotter. I must make sure my plants have enough water."

Felicity had an idea.

"If it's going to be really hot on Saturday, why don't we fly to Glitter Beach? It's always a bit cooler by the sea."

"Ooh yes!" exclaimed the fairies together. All except Polly.

Daisy noticed Polly looking worried.

"What's wrong, Pol?" she asked. "Don't you fancy splashing in the sea and wriggling your toes in the sand?"

Polly looked down at her feet and bit her lip. "Umm… er… I've got some homework to finish," she said.

The fairies looked at her in panic. Was there some homework they'd forgotten about? Polly was *always* the first to hand her homework in, whereas Felicity put off today anything she could do tomorrow.

"I thought I'd handed everything in!" said Daisy.

"Oh no!" groaned Holly, putting her head in her hands. "Not more work!"

"What homework haven't you finished?" asked Felicity.

Polly was still looking uncomfortable, and said vaguely, "Well, not homework exactly. I'm writing a story called *Toothy Tales*, just for fun."

Everyone knew Polly wanted to be a Tooth Fairy. She was the kind of fairy who was good at *everything* she tried. Polly had come top in history for remembering all the

...s fairies' names. In chemistry
...parkle dust had a twinkle no
other dust could match. And in
geography she could find countries
on the globe with her eyes closed.
But her real passion was smiles.
Toothy smiles, gappy
smiles, wide smiles,
tiny smiles, *any*
smiles!

"Thank goodness for that!"
exclaimed Felicity, relieved that her
day at the beach wouldn't be spoilt
by the thought of homework still to
do. "If it's for fun, then it won't have
a date to be handed in by – so you
can come to the beach after all!"

Polly still didn't look happy.

"It's quite a long flight to the beach and if it's hot we'll be really tired by the time we get there," she protested.

Daisy couldn't see a problem.

"I'm going to need to be up early to water all the plants," she said. "Let's *all* get up early and fly to the beach before it gets really hot."

"But we'll still have the journey back!" said Polly desperately.

This just wasn't like Polly at all, thought her friends. Polly was sensible, but she was always keen to do fun things. If they went cycling, the others would be pedalling off while Polly was still checking that her chain was fixed properly. Polly never started a recipe without checking she had all the ingredients first, whereas Felicity would get half-way through a recipe for chocolate cake before finding out she had no chocolate. And, even though Polly was brilliant at geography, she would look at the map *before* she set off, rather than wait until she got lost.

"Polly," said Felicity, putting her arm around her friend, "remember what a glorious day we had at the beach last year? We swam in the bay and ate oodles of pink sugary candy floss and..."

Felicity suddenly stopped. "I don't remember you coming last year, actually - but I can't remember why."

"You weren't feeling well," said Holly.

"That's final, then!" said Daisy. "You can't go another year without going to Glitter Beach! Forget your story. Don't worry about how long it will take to get there. Let's meet really early tomorrow morning and head for sun, sea and candy floss!"

Daisy had a big sun umbrella which she and Holly could carry between them. Felicity said she would make a picnic. Everyone was to bring their own towels, and Holly promised enough sun cream to share. Last year she had got rather burnt and was nicknamed Holly Berry for the rest of the summer!

Holly was going to stay the night at Felicity's house, so Daisy promised to knock on their door in the morning, on the way to pick up Polly. The plan was made!

✳ ✳ ✳

Polly couldn't sleep that night. The room was hot and she tossed and turned.

One o'clock.

Two o'clock.

Not even her favourite
pillow felt comfortable.

Just as she thought
she was drifting
off to sleep,
Polly woke
up with a
start.

Her heart was racing so fast she
could hear it beating.

She got up and went to the window.
The sky was full of tiny silver stars
and the moon seemed to be smiling
down at her.

"Oh Moon," she sighed. "How am
I going to tell my friends about my
terrible secret?"

* * *

Polly finally managed to fall asleep not long before she was due to get up.

In fact, she was still snuggled so deep under the covers when her friends arrived she didn't hear them ringing the front door bell.

Daisy flew up to Polly's bedroom window and tapped on the glass.

Still half-asleep, Polly tugged herself out of bed, rubbed her eyes and slowly went downstairs to open the front door.

When she saw the big beach umbrella, her tummy did a somersault. Today was the day!

"I don't feel well," she said in a feeble voice to her friends. "You have a lovely time at the beach. I think I'll just stay here at home."

"You're just sleepy. We felt horrible having to get up so early but we feel super now, don't we, Holly?" said Felicity, nudging Holly, who was

leaning against the doorframe yawning, her eyes half-shut.

Polly trudged back up the stairs to get dressed. Opening her cupboard she saw her purple, spotty swimming costume folded neatly on one of the shelves. Perhaps there was one last chance!

Grabbing the costume from the cupboard, she shouted downstairs to her friends, "There's a problem! I can't find my swimsuit. Go on without me!"

But before Polly had a chance to hide her costume under the mattress, Felicity had flown up the stairs and was standing in her bedroom.

Felicity was always amazed at how neat Polly's room was. All her wings

were freshly ironed and
hung neatly in the wardrobe.
Her jars of sparkle-dust were each
sealed with a tiny label and arranged
in order of strength. Her school wand
was lying on top of her school bag,
which was packed and ready for
Monday morning and, even though
Polly had only just got out of it, her
bed looked barely crumpled.

"You *are* sleepy!" laughed Felicity,
pointing at the purple swimsuit.
"Look! You're holding it!"

* * *

Little Blossoming glittered in the early
morning sun. As they flew over
the rooftops, the fairies could
see the town just beginning
to wake up below them.
Outside Sparkles,
their favourite café, a
fairy was putting out
tables and chairs.

Another fairy was delivering copies of the *Daily Flutter*, trying to push the newspapers through tiny letterboxes. Someone else was cycling slowly up Feather Hill, while two fairies jogged down it.

The friends flew over The School of Nine Wishes, with its golden gates, and across Nine Wish Wood, which belonged to the school.

Daisy could see her garden now, which was packed so full of flowers it looked like a huge burst of colour beneath them.

As they left Little Blossoming, the number of houses grew less and less, until they were flying over green fields which rolled out before them like a magical patchwork quilt, sloping gently down towards the sea.

And, finally, they saw Glitter Beach.

The beach looked just as they remembered it from last summer.

Golden
sands carpeted
the bay and swept round
in a huge semi-circle as if hugging
the shimmering sea. Where the sun
touched the sea it seemed as if tiny
silver stars were dancing on the water.

It really was beautiful.

* * *

Glitter Beach was already beginning
to get busy. Fairies were changing
behind towels, skipping back from
the shops with buckets and
spades, setting up stripy
deckchairs and throwing
open the shutters of

ice-cream-coloured beach huts.

The Water Fairies were walking
up and down the beach looking very
glamorous in their bright red costumes
and carrying their inflatable wings.

At the first sign of a fairy in trouble in the water, they could blow up their wings and head out into the sea.

Felicity had never actually seen any of them do this. Every time she had been to the beach they seemed to spend more time sitting on deckchairs by the 'Lost Fairy' sign drinking lemonade and eating ice-cream than rescuing fairies. Still, she was glad they were there.

Daisy and Felicity put up the sun umbrella and they all hung their wings from it. They wriggled into their swimming costumes, then laid their towels out on the sand.

"Last one in the water eats a sandy sandwich!" yelled Felicity, as she raced towards the sea, hotly pursued by Holly and Daisy.

Only Polly remained standing forlornly under the sun umbrella, her legs as wobbly as a jellyfish.

Any moment now, her friends
would turn and see her on the beach
and come running back to get her.

Carefully, Polly undid her wings,
hung them up with the others and,
taking a sandwich from the picnic
basket, crept away and hid behind
one of the beach huts.

"They'll probably think I've gone
to buy an ice-cream," she thought.

Felicity made huge splashes when she swam, so her friends tried to keep away from her. Holly swam with her head above the water, for fear of messing up her hair, while Daisy floated on her back, staring at the sky, and was carried along by the waves. After a few moments they realised that Polly was missing.

Daisy was sure that Polly had run into the sea with them.

"At least I *think* I'm sure," she said.

Felicity couldn't remember seeing Polly running down the beach, but thought she had been in the sea with them.

Holly pointed out that none of them would have been able to see whether she was there or not, with the amount of splashing Felicity had been doing!

The fairies' toes still touched the sand on the bottom, even though it felt like they'd been swimming out

to sea for ages, so they waded back
towards the beach.

"POLLY!" they all shouted. "POLLY,
WHERE ARE YOU?"

One of the Water Fairies approached
them.

"Is there a problem?" she asked.

"We've lost our friend!" said Felicity.
"We thought she might have been back
on the beach, but we can't see her."

"Look!" squealed Daisy. "Her wings!
Polly's wings are under the umbrella!
She'd never go anywhere other than
the sea without her wings. She *must*
have followed us into the water!"

Holly, who was worried about
Polly but was also enjoying the
drama, added, "But we don't
think she followed us out!"

There was no time to lose.
The Water Fairy leapt into
action. In an instant, her
wings inflated and she

ran towards the sea blowing a small silver whistle. The other Water Fairies began to scramble off their deckchairs and run down the beach and into the water.

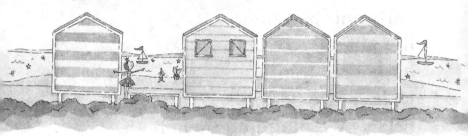

From behind the beach huts, Polly heard the whistle and popped her head around the corner. She could see Holly, Daisy and Felicity huddled together by the water's edge, and three Water Fairies flying rapidly across the beach, their wings inflating as they flew.

Suddenly she realised what was happening.

"They think I'm lost at sea and they're trying to rescue me!"

Polly darted out from behind the

hut and rushed towards her friends.

"I don't need saving!" she cried, running towards them.

The fairies turned towards her. Daisy's curly hair had gone flat, all the colour had gone from Holly's face and Felicity was hugging them both.

When she saw them, Polly burst into tears.

Felicity could barely get the words out for sobbing. "We thought... we thought you had *drowned*!"

The Water Fairies had noticed Polly return and one of them came up to the huddle of friends.

"Are you alright?" she asked Polly. "Where were you?"

"Hiding behind the beach huts," sobbed Polly, huge tears plopping into the sand.

"Why?" asked Felicity.

It was time to come clean. To own up to her secret. The thing that she had been keeping from her friends for years.

She, Polly, who was good at everything and never failed at anything, had never learnt to swim.

"You can't swim?" said Holly. "I wouldn't worry, lots of fairies are scared of water."

"I'm not scared of *water*," sniffed Polly. "I'm scared of *sinking*!"

Felicity hugged Polly. "Why didn't you *tell us*?"

"Everyone thinks I'm so good at everything, I was scared to admit there was something I couldn't do." Polly was still sobbing.

The Water Fairy put her arm around Polly.

"It's really important to learn how to swim. Even if *you* don't need rescuing, perhaps someone else will!"

"I know," sniffed Polly. "I just don't know where to start!"

"How about a lesson now, here with me on the beach?" said the Water Fairy. "We'll make you a Water Fairy for the day!"

Polly nodded enthusiastically.

And, with that, the Water Fairy handed Polly a pair of inflatable wings and led her into the water.

"Bet you an ice-cream Polly will end up being brilliant at swimming too!" said Felicity, before racing her fairy friends back to their towels.

And, as the three friends stretched out on the sand, under the shimmering sun, they could hear Polly giggling and splashing – happy in the water at last.

good friends won't mind
what you can
and can't do

as long as you're you!

Spooky Sleepover

During the lesson about 'Great Fairies in History', Felicity Wishes began to think about what she was going to do after school.

Tearing a tiny scrap of paper from her exercise book, she scribbled a note and passed it under the desk to Holly, who opened it, nodded, and passed it on to Daisy.

Daisy gave a little thumbs up sign and tried to pass it to Polly, but Polly was enjoying the lesson so much, she didn't

My house, after school, for chocolate cake? F xxx

notice Daisy pushing the note towards her across the desk.

Miss Fossil, the history teacher, did.

"Daisy, I do hope that note is extra information on the fairies we are studying," she said, picking up the folded piece of paper.

"If only I could grant wishes for myself," thought Daisy. "I could make myself disappear!"

Miss Fossil read the note, raised her eyebrows and, scrunching it into a ball, threw it into the wastepaper basket.

"I take it that you have all finished last week's history homework?" she asked, in a voice which meant she knew they hadn't even started.

"Nine o'clock tomorrow morning I expect to see a large pile of books on my desk!"

History homework! They'd forgotten all about it.

✳ ✳ ✳

Felicity, Holly, Daisy and Polly
huddled together under the large
oak tree in the playing field during
break.

"That was *sooo* embarrassing,"
said Daisy.

"I was looking forward to you all
coming round and eating chocolate
cake," said Felicity. She'd baked the
cake yesterday and, by the time she'd
covered it in thick, dark, gooey icing,
the burnt bits hardly showed at all.

Holly was beginning to panic.

"What about this homework?

I haven't even started it and it's due in tomorrow!"

"Don't get your wings in a twist, Hol," said Felicity, as she reached into her bag and pulled out her exercise book. "All we have to do is write about a famous fairy. It can't be *that* difficult."

After she had removed a piece of bubble gum which was stuck to the cover, shaken out the crumbs from a half-eaten biscuit, and leafed through a dozen doodle-filled pages, Felicity finally found the instructions for their homework.

"Choose one important fairy in history. In your own words, describe why this fairy has made a difference to the lives of modern fairies," read Felicity.

"What are we going to *do*?" shrieked Holly.

Polly, who had been busy reading a book and munching an apple, looked up calmly.

"Go to the school library, find books on fairy history, read them, choose a fairy, then write about her. That's what I did."

Holly, Daisy and Felicity looked at Polly in astonishment.

"You mean," said Felicity, "you've already *done* the homework?"

"Mmmm," mumbled Polly, her mouth full of apple.

"Goody – we can copy it!" said Holly, flinging her arms in the air in relief.

"I've handed it in," said Polly, still munching.

"And you didn't *tell* us?" asked Daisy.

"I knew I couldn't leave it until the

last minute,"
replied Polly.
"I'm out
tonight."
"What!
Where?
Who with?"
chorused
her friends.

"I asked Pearl, one of the Tooth
Fairies, whether I could come out
with her tonight and see a proper
Tooth Fairy in action. I won't be
home until very late."

The other fairies were impressed.
Polly was taking her decision to
become a Tooth Fairy *very* seriously.

Felicity had an idea.

"Why don't we all go the library,
then go back to my house and do
our homework together!"

Daisy wasn't sure.

"If we spend the evening chatting

and eating cake, I don't think we'll have time to finish it. We'll be up all night!"

"Perfect!" cried Felicity. "We can have a sleepover! It won't matter *what* time we finish if you stay at my house."

"Are you *sure* you can't come?" Holly asked Polly, secretly hoping that even though Polly had done her homework, she might be persuaded to stay at Felicity's as well. That way, if they got stuck, Polly could help them.

Polly shook her head. "Count me out. I'll definitely either be too late or too tired to join you."

* * *

It was so long since any of them had been to the School Library, that Felicity, Holly and Daisy managed to get lost in the corridors and found themselves flying in totally the wrong direction towards Fairy Godmother's office, just as she was flying out.

"What are you young fairies up to?" she asked.

"We're off to the library, Fairy Godmother," said Felicity.

"We want to get on with our history project," added Daisy.

"How lovely," thought Fairy Godmother to herself as she flew off to yet another staff meeting. "What a change to find fairies who are eager to do their homework instead of leaving it until the last minute!"

* * *

The library shelves were bursting with books on every subject. The fairies stood in a group, looking bewildered.

A crown appeared over the top of a pile of books, followed by a huge pair of glasses. They belonged to Miss Page, the school librarian. Although Miss Page liked the young fairies to

enjoy reading, she *didn't*
like them messing up her
neat shelves by not
putting the books
they had borrowed
back in the right
place.

"Could you help
us find information
on famous fairies?"
Felicity asked Miss Page,
showing her the homework question.

Miss Page shuddered at the sight
of Felicity's crumpled exercise book.
She pointed them towards the history
shelves.

"*Please* be careful," she pleaded.
"Some of those books are *very* old!"

* * *

Looking through the books, Felicity
and her friends found reading about
famous fairies much more fun than
they had imagined. There were tales

of fairies who had made solo flights across the desert or flown to the brightest stars in the sky. They read about a fairy who invented wings which could be powered by sunshine, and a famous fairy poet who always spoke in rhyme, even when she wasn't writing poems!

Felicity decided to write about a fairy called Lucy Sunshine, who had been at the School of Nine Wishes many years ago. Lucy was the first fairy to make powdered summer sun, a vital ingredient in modern sparkle dust. Without Lucy's work, sparkle dust could only be produced in very small quantities.

Daisy was getting very excited reading about famous Blossom Fairies and was scribbling excitedly in her notebook.

"Did you know that the first known Blossom Fairy was called Rose Petal?"

she asked Holly and Felicity. "She was the fairy who discovered the everlasting lily."

Holly was finding it difficult to choose a famous fairy to write about. They were all interesting, but which one had made the most difference to the life of a modern fairy like Holly?

Just then, Holly's mobile phone
rang.

Felicity and Daisy gasped and
ducked behind the shelves. They were
not supposed to use their phones in
school and *never* in the library.

Holly tried to turn it off, but it was
too late. Miss Page had seen her and,
from the way she was flying, Holly
knew she was in BIG trouble.

"Please give me that phone," she
whispered sharply to Holly. "You can
collect it from me this time tomorrow."

"Twenty-four hours without
my phone!" whispered Holly.
"What *am* I going to do?"

"What did people do before phones?" said Felicity. "Whoever invented them really made a difference to our lives!"

"That's it!" exclaimed Holly. "*That's* who I will write about. The fairy who invented the telephone!"

In the middle of *The History of the Fairy World, Part 3*, they found the inventor of the fairy phone, Scarlet Belle.

"Thank goodness for Scarlet!" they whispered to each other as they pushed the books back on the shelves, gathered up their notes, pens and pencils, and, to the relief of Miss Page, left the library.

* * *

At Felicity's house, surrounded by chocolate cake and fizzy lemonade, the fairy friends settled down to finish their homework.

Felicity had trouble starting hers. She looked at the question on the paper and the notes she had made in the library.

She copied the question neatly into her exercise book, drew a line under it and made a smiley face for a full stop.

She chewed on the end of her pen, rearranged the coloured pencils in the order of the colours of the rainbow and watched her friends scribbling away.

"If Lucy Sunshine can make powdered summer sun, then surely I can manage to do my homework!" thought Felicity, as she began to write.

By the time they had all finished their homework, it was dark and windy outside and pouring with rain.

"I'm feeling really sleepy," yawned Daisy, who was already in her nightie and was sitting on Felicity's bed, her toes tucked under the pink covers.

"I feel tired too," said Felicity. Her eyelids felt so heavy they needed matchsticks to prop them up.

Felicity and Daisy snuggled down at one end of the bed and Holly tucked herself in at the other. They were too tired to even tickle each other's toes. But the moment Felicity turned out the light, she felt wide-awake.

While the other two slept, Felicity listened to the roar of the wind and the lashing of the rain against the window.

Lying very still, so as not to wake Daisy and Holly, Felicity's gaze rested

on the gap below the blind, where she
could see the moon shining, filling the
room with a misty white light.

Suddenly the moon disappeared,
and the room became pitch black.

Felicity's heart began to beat faster
and faster. Then, from outside, came
a long, low, moaning noise.

"Are you awake?" Felicity whispered
to Daisy, who continued to snore
gently beside her.

Felicity wriggled her toes at the
bottom of the bed and tickled Holly.
"Are you awake, Holly?"

"Mmm…" replied Holly sleepily.

"Can you hear that noise…that
moaning noise?"

"It's just the wind," muttered Holly, rolling over.

"Holly, listen!" whispered Felicity. "There's something out there!"

"It's just the wind, Felicity," Holly said. "Unless... it's The Thing!"

Felicity sat bolt upright in bed. "What thing?"

By this time Daisy was awake too, so Felicity switched on the light.

"What's going on?" asked Daisy, rubbing her eyes.

"Holly said that moaning noise is a thing," squeaked Felicity.

Holly sat up in bed and pulled the covers about her.

"Not *a* thing," she said in a low menacing whisper. "*The* Thing! No one has ever seen The Thing. But they know when it's there."

"H-h-h-ow?" gasped Felicity, who had pulled the covers right up over her nose so only her scared, wide eyes were peeping over the top.

"Because it moans and it wails and even the moon hides when it's near!"

Felicity remembered the moon disappearing, and pulled the covers right over her head.

At that moment there was another groaning and creaking sound, like a rusty, old pair of wings.

"Has it gone?" Daisy whispered. "Has The Thing gone?"

Holly was enjoying herself.

"The Thing never leaves. Wherever you hide, The Thing will get you!"

Felicity and Daisy were now really frightened and, even though she had started the story as a bit of fun, Holly also began to feel scared.

"Where does it stay when it's here?" asked Felicity, her voice trembling.

"It's downstairs," squeaked Daisy in a high-pitched whisper. "Listen!"

"It's just a joke," said Holly, her

tummy doing somersaults as she
clutched the bedding around her. "I
mean, I was just pretending. There's
no such thing as The Thing."

But even Holly couldn't fail to miss
the sound coming from downstairs.

Tap. Tap. Tap.

"It's the wind," she said, trying to
convince herself.

"The wind doesn't make that sort
of noise!" said Felicity under her
breath. "It's The Thing!"

The tapping stopped.

Holly sank back on to the bed. The moon seemed to be laughing at her from behind the blind.

"I'm going to pull the blind down tightly and then let's get to sleep," she said, as she tiptoed her way to the window.

Just as she touched the blind – "ARRGHH!" – she leapt back from the window, white as a snowdrop and shaking like a jelly.

"What is it?" cried Felicity.

"Is it The Thing?" screamed Daisy, as Holly dived back under the bedclothes.

"A face... I saw a face..." Holly gasped.

All three friends hid under the covers and hugged each other tightly.

The tapping noise started again, followed by an eerie howl. It seemed to be closer than ever.

Felicity was more frightened than she had ever been in her life, but feeling her friends shaking with fear beside her suddenly made her feel much braver. They needed her to be strong.

"Are you *sure* that you made up the story about The Thing?" she asked Holly in the dark of the bedclothes.

"Y-y-ess," said Holly, her teeth chattering with fright.

Tap Tap Tap went the noise.

It was getter faster and faster.

Felicity slowly poked her head out from under the bedclothes, but kept her eyes tightly shut.

The tapping had suddenly become much louder.

BANG BANG BANG it went.

Finding courage she didn't know she had, Felicity opened her eyes and went over to the window with wobbly legs. Taking a deep breath she flung up the blind. And what she saw there gave her a tremendous shock!

Banging on the window and shouting "Let me in!" was Polly!

* * *

"There weren't many teeth to collect this evening, so I decided to pop by and join the sleepover!" said Polly, climbing through the window and shaking the rain from her wings.

"I tried to knock on the door downstairs but no-one heard me, so I flew up and tried knocking on the window."

"We didn't hear you," said Felicity, handing her a towel. "We had our heads under the covers!"

"But you saw me, Holly," said Polly. "Why didn't you let me in?"

"She thought you were The Thing," said Daisy.

"My turn to make the hot chocolate, I think!" said Holly, heading towards the kitchen, her cheeks bright pink with embarrassment. "And then you can tell us all about your night, Polly!"

the most scary
thing about
being frightened

is what you
imagine.

Cooking Crisis

Felicity Wishes and her friends were making their way home from school. They were talking about the lessons they'd had that day.

Suddenly, Felicity remembered something *much* more exciting.

"Polly! There's only a couple of days left until your birthday and you *still* haven't decided whether or not to have a party!"

Holly, who had been flying along while trying to read a magazine at the same time, crashed into

Daisy, who had stopped to smell some pink roses.

"I've been too busy to even think about my birthday," Polly told Felicity, as she helped untangle Holly and Daisy. "I suppose I should do *something*."

"Leave it to me!" said Felicity brightly. "I'll make you a yummy birthday cake. In fact, *lots* of scrummy birthday cakes!"

The fairies looked at each other with raised eyebrows and wide eyes. It wasn't that Felicity didn't cook. She *loved* to cook. It was just that she never stuck to a recipe! Sometimes she forgot to read the recipe all the way through before starting, or found she didn't have all the ingredients, or forgot to switch the oven on. Something *always* seemed to go wrong.

Felicity saw her friends looking at

her in an 'are you sure this is a good idea?' kind of way.

"Don't worry!" she said. "Come to my house on Saturday at four o'clock for a birthday tea!"

With a hop, skip and a flip of her wings, Felicity flew off to plan Polly's birthday tea.

"I'll pop round early," said Daisy to the others. "*Someone* has got to keep an eye on her!"

* * *

All day on Friday during school, Felicity thought about what she was going to bake.

"Are you *sure* you want to do this, Felicity?" asked Polly, after Felicity had questioned her for the hundredth time about whether she preferred jam or cream, or both, in a sponge cake. "I'm happy to go to Ice-Cream Dreams if it's too much bother."

"It's all under control!" Felicity told Polly, writing down another cake idea on her ever-increasing list.

* * *

Felicity had taken a big pile of cookery books to bed with her and had marked the recipes with little slips of pink paper. It had taken her ages to fall asleep and, when she finally did, she dreamt she'd fallen into a giant bowl of cake mixture and eaten too much to climb out!

When she woke the next day, not only was it later than she had planned, but all the little pink slips of paper had fallen out of the cookery books, as she'd fallen asleep with them on her bed.

"Never mind," she thought to

herself. "I'm sure I can remember the recipes. I've read them so many times!"

She looked at the list of cakes to bake. She would have to work quickly if she was to get everything finished by four o'clock!

* * *

Felicity switched on the oven.

"I'll leave it to heat up for ten minutes," she thought to herself. "Then I'll start making the chocolate birthday cake."

She wandered out into the garden, just as Holly was flying past. Seeing Felicity, she stopped to chat.

"I'm off to have my hair done,"

said Holly. "I thought I might try Star Treatment for a change."

Holly and Felicity were still chatting about hairstyles when Holly wrinkled her nose.

"Can you smell burning?" she asked Felicity. "Have you got anything in the oven?"

"Not yet," replied Felicity. "I wonder if someone is having a bonfire?"

The burning smell became stronger and stronger.

"Are you *sure* it's not something you're cooking?" said Holly, setting off down the path to Felicity's house.

"It's really not me!" laughed Felicity, following her. "I've nothing in the oven to burn!"

They trooped into Felicity's kitchen. Thick black smoke was pouring from behind the oven door.

"Don't open the door!" shouted Holly. "Turn off the oven and open

the windows!"

Holly and Felicity stood staring at the smouldering oven. When the smoke had died down, Felicity carefully opened the door and peered inside. Wearing a huge pair of oven gloves she reached in and brought out a small, black object.

"What is it?" asked Holly, poking it with a wooden spoon.

"I think it *was* a gingerbread fairy. I must have left it in the oven by mistake last time I baked!" said Felicity. "Look, you can just about make out the outline of her crown!"

* * *

Holly left to go to Star Treatment and Felicity began to make the chocolate cake. The oven was still very hot.

"Most people have to wait for the oven to heat up before they start cooking," she thought to herself as she stirred the cake mixture. "Trust me to have to wait for it to cool down!"

The cake mixture was creamy and golden. Time to add the chocolate powder! She looked in the cupboard but couldn't see any.

"I *know* it's in here," she thought as she peered at the tins and packets.

Eventually, at the back, she found
what she was looking for. But, when
she prised open the lid, instead of
seeing a loose mound of chocolate
powder, all she saw was a solid,
brown lump. Felicity looked at the
'Use By' date on the bottom of the

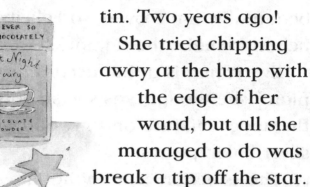

tin. Two years ago!
She tried chipping
away at the lump with
the edge of her
wand, but all she
managed to do was
break a tip off the star.
Hot water didn't even *begin*
to dissolve it, and banging the tin
on the floor to free the chocolate only
dented it.

Felicity glanced at the clock. The
morning was nearly over! There wasn't
time to go to Little Blossoming for
more chocolate powder. She'd have
to turn the mixture into fairy cakes.

She was sure Polly wouldn't mind.

Just as she was about to spoon the mixture into pretty paper cases she decided to add more self-raising flour, just for luck.

* * *

The fairy cake mixture was rising beautifully in the oven, so Felicity began to make the flapjacks.

"Everything is going according to plan!" she thought, as she smoothed the gooey mixture on to two large, silver baking trays.

"This is better," she thought, as she took the golden fairy cakes out of the oven and left them on a rack to cool.

Putting the flapjacks in the oven, she set the timer for fifteen minutes and, as there were no more bowls left to make the cherry cookies, began to do the washing up, her arms elbow deep in frothy bubbles.

Out of the corner of her eye she

noticed something about the rack of cooling fairy cakes had changed. Instead of twelve cakes, there were now only eleven. She was *sure* she had filled twelve cases, but perhaps she had been mistaken. A moment later, she looked again. This time there were only ten!

Puzzled, Felicity stared at the cakes. In front of her eyes, one by one, the cakes rose up and floated out of the open window and across the garden.

She had put so much self-raising flour in the mixture they were floating away as they cooled!

Felicity rushed out into the garden and ran down the path, but it was too late. The cakes were heading off over Little Blossoming.

Just when Felicity thought it couldn't get any worse, she remembered the flapjacks. The kitchen timer had gone off, but Felicity had been right at the bottom of the garden, so hadn't heard it!

Dashing back into the house, she opened the oven door and pulled out two trays of solid, burnt flapjacks, stuck firmly to their tins.

Felicity sat at the kitchen table and buried her head in her hands.

"What *am* I going to do?" she wailed.

"Go to the cake shop!" said a voice.

Felicity looked up to see Daisy staring at the chaos that surrounded her distraught fairy friend.

"What are you doing here?" asked Felicity, drying her eyes on the oven glove.

"There's a trail of fairy cakes floating over Little Blossoming," said Daisy, prodding the burnt flapjacks. "I guessed they came from your house."

* * *

Felicity agreed with Daisy that if the birthday tea was to go ahead, there was no choice but to go to the cake shop, but when they arrived at The Sticky Bun, there wasn't a single cake to be seen.

"Aren't there *any* cakes left?"
Felicity asked the shop assistant
desperately.

The assistant shook her head.

"Someone came in and bought
every cake, bun and biscuit we had."

* * *

Daisy and Felicity left the shop and
sat underneath a huge tree.

Felicity had one last idea.

"Daisy, would you try and wish for
some cakes for me?" She hesitated
for a moment, remembering her
fairy motto. "You would be using
your wishes for the good of others."

But Daisy didn't want to try.

"Remember when I tried to magic
some scones in cookery class?" she
asked Felicity. "They were as heavy
and as hard as stones."

Holly claimed her toe still hurt
from where a scone had fallen on it.

"Owww!" screeched Felicity.

"Yes, that's what Holly said," remembered Daisy.

"No, I mean, ouch, I've just been hit by a falling apple!"

The fairies looked up and realised they were sitting under an apple tree bursting with apples.

"Toffee apples!" exclaimed Felicity. "We can make Polly toffee apples!"

Daisy flew up into the tree and gently tapped on the branches with her wand, and Felicity stood below, holding out her skirt to catch the falling fruit.

"I don't suppose you've got any lollipop sticks?" asked Daisy.

"Hundreds!" said Felicity, remembering a drawer full of them at home. "I knew they'd come in handy one day!"

* * *

When they got back to Felicity's kitchen they washed the apples, pushed in the lolly sticks and, after checking one of Felicity's recipe books, made a huge pot of sticky toffee mixture into which they dipped the apples.

"Thank goodness *something* has gone right!" said Felicity, admiring the rows of apples dripping with gleaming, glassy toffee.

It was nearly four o'clock! Soon Polly and Holly would be round.

Felicity and Daisy put out Polly's presents and cards on the table and filled jugs with lemonade.

Felicity's tummy began to rumble.

"In all the rush I forgot to have lunch!" she said to Daisy.

"Why not try a toffee apple?" said Daisy. "There are plenty of them!"

Felicity picked up one of the apples and sunk her teeth through the sticky toffee and into the crispy apple. But when she tried to take another bite she found that the toffee was so sticky her teeth had become stuck. The harder she tried to pull the toffee apple from her mouth, the more the toffee set around her teeth.

"Is that nice?" asked Daisy, looking at the apples and not noticing Felicity, wide-eyed and pointing frantically at her mouth.

Felicity let out a muffled noise which sounded like "Mmmmm".

"In that case, I'll try one myself," said Daisy. As she bit into the sticky apple she turned and saw Felicity, her mouth stuck to the toffee apple, trying to tell her not to eat one. Too late!

The fairies tried to pull the apples out but, every time they did, they felt as if their teeth were coming out.

The phone rang. Felicity picked it up.

"Uuh – ho," she said.

"Felicity! It's Polly. I'm going to be a little late. Are you all right?"

Felicity tried to say yes but it came out as "us".

Polly was worried now.

"Is Daisy there? Put me on to Daisy."

Felicity handed the phone to Daisy, who managed to make a series of muffled grunts and snorts before putting the phone down.

* * *

Polly came flying through the door at great speed.

She could not believe her eyes when she saw her two friends sitting at the kitchen table, silent, with two huge toffee apples stuck in their mouths.

As it was Felicity's kitchen and

involved Felicity's cooking, she didn't even ask how it had happened. Very gently, she tugged at the sticky apples in her friends' mouths, ignoring their yelps and carefully chipping away any bits of stuck toffee. Eventually, Daisy and Felicity were freed from their sticky apples.

"You're going to be a brilliant Tooth Fairy!" exclaimed Felicity, gulping down a glass of lemonade. "I thought my teeth were going to be stuck to that toffee apple for ever!"

"Thank goodness I stopped at The Sticky Bun for cakes!" said Holly, coming through the door with a box filled with the most yummy cakes and buns they had ever seen.

"It was *you*!" said Felicity to Holly. "You were the one who bought all the cakes! How did you know that I had had a bad cooking day?"

"I saw the fairy cakes flying across Little Blossoming this morning," said Holly, sticking some candles into one of the cakes. "I thought these might come in useful."

Polly saw Felicity's face crumple a little and put her arms around her.

"Holly buying cakes was a lovely gesture but" – she winked at Holly – "you trying to make them yourself for me is every bit as lovely. It's the thought that counts."

"Don't worry," said Felicity brightly, "I'll have it all under control next year!"

things given with
all your heart
are always lovely

even when they
go wrong!

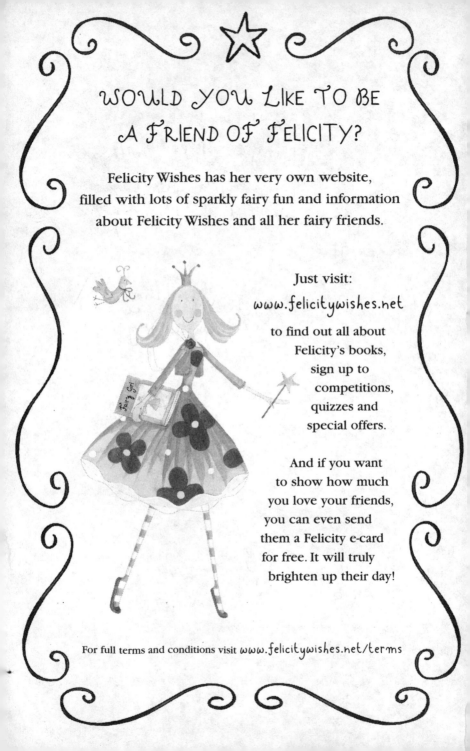

WOULD YOU LIKE TO BE A FRIEND OF FELICITY?

Felicity Wishes has her very own website,
filled with lots of sparkly fairy fun and information
about Felicity Wishes and all her fairy friends.

Just visit:
www.felicitywishes.net

to find out all about
Felicity's books,
sign up to
competitions,
quizzes and
special offers.

And if you want
to show how much
you love your friends,
you can even send
them a Felicity e-card
for free. It will truly
brighten up their day!

For full terms and conditions visit www.felicitywishes.net/terms